SWOLE: FLEX FRIDAY

Published and written by: Golden Czermak
1st Edition

WARNING: This is a **short story** written for mature readers. It is pure

escapism, containing adult themes, coarse language, erotic sexual

situations, male-male sex, and nudity.

SWOLE
FLEX FRIDAY

ACKNOWLEDGEMENTS

Here we are at the end of this fun short story series. I want to take a moment to thank my readers of this short series and my full-length novels. Without you, this wouldn't be nearly as rewarding. Thank you for helping to bring Trent, Jared, and Jonny to life by joining them on this peculiar week of gym life, squats, hot dog buns, soap, and hot man-on-man sex.

This isn't goodbye, it's just until the next time!

CHAPTER 1

FEISTY

JONNY CAMERON DIDN'T LIKE BEING inside Swole during the day. Yet there he was, loitering near the line of treadmills positioned at the front of the gym. He was waiting on Trent Cassidy, who was finishing some paperwork for a new client who had just signed on.

"A six-month term!" he'd beamed while departing with her for his office. His smile was filled with sincere happiness.

The woman happened to be a buxom blonde wearing an over-tight top that strained against her fake tits and shorts that were sucked deep into her ass crack. The outfit screamed, 'Attention all men! Attention all men! Make sure to stare lustfully at me but don't let me catch you, because I'll be sure to call you out for being a pervert!'

Trent would sign up someone like her right away, Jonny thought bitterly. *Must maintain that reputation after all…*

Although Jonny had a hard time with it, he couldn't fault Trent for signing up his brand of clientele. They were helping the man out, the large amounts of business his gym was pulling in each month was a testament to that. But logical things like revenue were inconvenient facts, so Jonny ignored them. Opting to be a tad jealous instead, it was rather silly of him to be resentful. By the same time tomorrow, he'd be on a bus, pulling into the town of Marshall. Back home and wallowing in sober reality.

Woo fucking hoo, thank you very much!

Speaking of reality, perhaps that's why Jonny didn't like being in the gym at that time of day. Up until now, he'd been there near closing time or after dark with Trent. There were no other people there to spoil the fun; they could do what they wanted away from prying, judgmental eyes. During the night hours, the heat of their bodies, sweating flesh, and tangled bodies made for an intimate, magical experience. However, under the scornful sun, the whole place took on a different vibe. Hot sweat collecting on the equipment became arrestingly gross, the smells of dirty people wrenching, and their bodies hairy, acne-ridden, and wrinkled in the unflattering light. The sun made the fantasy distant if not broken, Jonny was longing to experience it again. But that wasn't to be, at least for some time. They were not going to be at the gym tonight.

Impatient and hungry, Jonny glanced toward a clock made from an old weight plate. It was hanging on a maroon wall, perched precariously on two hefty nails. Eleven-twenty was the time and Jonny assumed (more hoping) that Trent would be done within the next ten minutes so they could grab a bite to eat.

There were a few small cafés next door and any one of those would suit Jonny and his complaining stomach just fine. Anywhere but Sir Mixalot, which was situated down at the far end of the strip mall. That place became very special after last night, when the two of them were ordering smoothies along with Jared Hughes. Everything in their odd, little triangle came together from that moment, so it wouldn't feel right if they were to go without him.

There was no sign of Trent when Jonny's stomach rumbled at eleven-thirty. No Trent still when it growled again at a quarter to twelve.

Where the fuck are you, T-bag? Jonny thought, Jared's nickname the only thing preventing him from getting completely livid.

Just as Jonny's stomach began to gurgle one more time, sounding like a freight train filled with a cargo of roaring bears, Trent was bounding toward him in his training attire.

"I am *so* sorry, Jonny," Trent said, genuinely apologetic.

It caught Jonny off guard just like Trent's incoming arm, which grabbed hold of him at the shirt collar.

Trent yanked him close, giving him a gentle kiss on the forehead.

As Jonny pulled slightly away, Trent's hand was messing up his hair.

"What's gotten into you?" Jonny asked suspiciously.

"I'm just in a fan-fucking-tastic mood, my man," Trent answered, grinning like a Cheshire cat. "Get this: she just signed up for a full year! She also paid for the *entire thing* up front *and* has five other friends that are going to come by after the first few weeks of training!" His emerald eyes grew a few karats. "Jackpot!"

Jonny's gaze scurried away, his brown eyes like a couple of rats escaping trouble.

"Sounds like you're going to be really busy making some good first impressions." His voice was cheery yet dry. An undercurrent of resentment flowed with the words. He was still looking away when Trent replied.

"Yeah, it's going to be busy." Trent placed a hand on Jonny's shoulder. "But not too busy to overlook my Jonny-boy. You must be starving, by the way."

"How can you tell?" Jonny asked, turning around.

"You and your stomach are being quite feisty."

Feisty? Jonny thought. *More like famished!*

"It's all good man," Trent said. "We'll head next door to Bruno's. Their wraps are to die for."

"Let's hope it doesn't come to that point."

"What, you dying?" Trent chuckled, saying, "Well, it won't from being gluttonous that's for sure. Their portions aren't massive so it won't be too heavy. Which is a good thing considering we have an arm session to knock out afterward."

Smiling, Jonny took a few steps toward the door, then stopped dead in his tracks. His face became one big grimace.

"Um, what?"

"You really need to get your hearing checked out," Trent said, pushing Jonny toward the door. "I said we had an arm workout; it's the only routine we have left to do this week."

Jonny looked at the all the cars in the parking lot, their dirty chassis and windows glistening user the sun. There were so many of them, which meant there were a lot of people. He gulped.

"W-we're g-going to w-workout n-now?" Jonny stuttered. "A r-regular one or one of y-your s-special ones?"

Trent shrugged indifferently.

"I dunno. That depends on you and your fight or flight instincts."

"Holy shit," Jonny muttered, leaning toward flight. *He can't be serious, can he?*

Jonny must have forgotten who he was thinking about. Since when had Trent *not* been serious, and since when did he care about who saw?

Jesus Christ… Jesus Christ… Jesus…

"Hey, don't worry," Trent said as the door shut behind him, cutting off the busy noise of the gym. The sounds were replaced by those of spring, along with a warm breeze and the smell of fresh cut grass from the median. "The gym will be relatively dead by the time we finish eating."

Jonny looked back inside. It looked packed to him.

"You sure about that?"

"I better be," Trent laughed. "I do own the place. With this being more of a younger, college gym we have a schedule you could set a watch to."

Jonny and Trent headed toward Bruno's café while Trent explained, trying to ease Jonny's frazzled nerves.

"Mondays are easily the busiest day of the week, packed beyond belief with those that have to get their swole on. More than likely they're doing chest, too, since people subconsciously judge a man's strength by the size of his chest and arms. Over the weekend nobody even gave the gym a second thought, focused more on beer and good times. Not that there's anything wrong with that… it keeps them coming and my pockets full."

Jonny nodded, turning back when he heard the beat from the energetic gym music. A couple of ladies were leaving, followed by an attractive Mexican guy.

"Tuesdays," Trent continued, "aren't as busy but those that stick around are doing some other kind of routine. Be it push and pull, or back versus chest, or whatever. Wednesdays, the attendance is cut roughly in half. You won't see that many Logan University students as they're catching up on coursework that's due or some other campus-related thing.

They always pick Wednesday for some reason. Those that are in are the career crowd, coming before and after work *or*, like the woman that signed up today, those with time on their hands and money to burn."

"You mean the cougar? Lucky you," Jonny said, smirking.

"You bet," Trent said, twitching his eyebrows to and fro. "That brings us to the downward spiral. Thursdays are nearly dead with only a quarter of the regular members coming in. Most won't be there because they don't want to be too sore for any fun on Friday night. Gotta be ready to swing a mean right hook when your girlfriend gets hit on, right? Which brings us to today, where you normally see the hardcore members like Will Marsh – the big son of a bitch you saw the other night – coming in." Trent paused when Jonny's face broke out in a weird mix of intrigue and fear. He couldn't tell which was more prominent. "That's why I close earlier on Friday, Saturday, and Sunday," he continued. "No point in staying open late when everyone's out enjoying themselves and showing off their gains over the weekend. But it makes sure the loop starts right over again on international chest day."

They reached Bruno's and Jonny peeked in. It was a casual eatery with a 1950s vibe. Trent stepped ahead and held the door open.

"So, you're telling me hardly anyone will be in there when we get back?" Jonny asked.

"Yes. Most leave around lunch time. Just the hardcore dudes will be there, but most will come later in the day. Trent had a flash of reverent awe on his face. "Those freaks of nature get made fun of a lot for having small dicks and gross appearances. The former is a myth, by the way. Those guys may run enough juice to make a bull horny, but their dicks stay the same size. It's because most of their legs get to over thirty inches around so their third legs look small in comparison. It's an illusion… trust me, *I know*. That said, I'm not speaking about their balls. Those suckers definitely go the way of the dinosaurs injecting that much test."

"Why do they want to get so huge?" Jonny asked, unable to imagine why anyone would want their nuts to shrivel up like dried beans. As he stepped inside the café, the smell of food was heavenly.

"Simple: because they can," Trent said plainly. "Goals for me, right?"

Jonny laughed because he thought Trent was perfect the way he was. Trent, like most bodybuilders, did not.

"Those guys dwarf me," he continued, "and as far as their gross appearances go, many take that as a complement and wear that shit like a badge of honor. It takes a lot of work no matter if you're on steroids or not so I can at least respect that. It's not like they give a fuck about what anyone thinks anyway."

"That's just like you," Jonny said.

"Exactly! Just like your boy Trent. As much as I respect it that kind of muscle has fringe benefits, too."

Jonny was almost afraid to ask, reaching the counter.

"Next please," said the friendly server.

Trent leaned in and whispered, "It's hot as fuck to rub on with your hands… or your tongue."

AS ALLUDED TO, THE MEAL was great and once the two of them returned to Swole, it resembled a ghost town. All that was missing were tumbleweeds bouncing through the cardio section.

Trent looked Jonny over briefly to make sure his workout attire was appropriate. Once he was satisfied that his red sneakers, dark gray shorts, and loose white tee were sufficient, he made way for a smaller room adjacent to the tanning booths. Part of Jonny was hoping to catch a glimpse of Will in the leg room as they walked by, but sadly he wasn't in there.

"Later on, over the weekend," Trent said.

"Huh?"

"Will," he clarified. "I see you looking for the big guy. He does legs twice a week so it'll be Saturday when he's in here next for those. He's got shoulders tonight I think and my lightweight ass plans to be far away. Bastard does at least seventies for front raises. Freak."

Jonny was amazed; that was more than double the weight of the dumbbells Trent had been using.

Opening the door, Trent welcomed Jonny into one of the smaller personal training parlors. They were set up so trainers could get more undivided attention from their clients, who would feel less intimidated within the walls. Moving the single seated bench over to the center of the room, he bid Jonny to sit in it.

"Okay, we'll start with seated curls," Trent said, grabbing two twenty pound dumbbells. He set them on the floor in front of Jonny before returning for a couple of fifties for himself. "So, what you're going to do is take one in each hand then slowly curl it up and slightly out, like this.

Pause for a second or two at the top where you're going to squeeze and then lower it to the floor."

Jonny and Trent performed four amazing sets, their arms starting to swell with blood, teasing other body parts to follow suit. From seated curls, they performed supersets of hammer curls with skull crushers, used a set of cables set up in the corner for twenty-ones and rope press-downs, then returned to the seated bench to start on overhead triceps extensions.

Trent was a sweaty mess, large veins protruding up the length of his forearms, over his biceps, and into his shoulders.

"Okay so for these," he said between pants, "you're going to…"

"Uh. Excuse me," a terse voice cut in. "I was on that."

Trent set his weights down and turned. He was staring at a man dressed in baggy shorts covered with dark patches of sweat. He had an irritated look on his face, towel draped around his neck while curly black hairs nearly touched it in the back. His looks reminded Trent of a dirty armpit, the arrogance wafting off him like BO.

"*What* was that?" Trent responded, not taking his eyes off the man.

The panting was also gone, causing Jonny to gulp loudly.

"I said I was using that bench." The man's tone had escalated too, trying to out-man Trent.

After glancing at the time, Trent patted Jonny on the shoulder and stood upright. He strode over to the man, back spread wide like a cobra, stopping just before their chests touched. He was close enough to kiss him, but didn't because the BO he imagined earlier was real. Nauseatingly real. Instead Trent leaned forward, trying not to gag as he spoke.

"Let me make something clear. If you leave a piece of equipment at a gym, especially my gym, to go chat up a girl, to take a massive shit, or to play how many strokes does it take to get my dick to pop off, you are no longer "on" that piece of equipment. So, if you come up to me after half an hour doing any one or all those things – smell of pussy on your lips, cum on your fingers, or toilet paper stuck to your goddamn shoes – just to say, 'I was on that,' I'll be more than happy to tell you to go fuck yourself and have a nice day."

Was Trent really speaking to a member like that? Jonny asked himself. Regardless, he found it hot, just like the back of Trent's ears, now blazing red.

The man started to say something back (his upper lip quivering) but backed down a second later. Snatching the towel off his neck, it made a whipping noise and he patted his forehead gently with it. Turning, the man left without so much as saying another word.

"Be sure to have a nice day," Trent called as the door slammed closed.

"Damn!" Jonny said, unable to suppress the gray tent erecting itself in his crotch. "Who was that?"

"That douche? He's a pain in my ass, and not the good kind," Trent answered, returning to Jonny's side. He glanced down, now with a smirk on this face. "Now, where were we? Oh yeah, triceps…"

Trent didn't get to say anything else. Jonny had sprung to his feet, their lips colliding. His dick was hard, pressing painfully against Trent's.

"God damn I'm gonna miss you," Jonny said briskly, resuming the fervent kiss.

"There's still plenty of time," Trent said, latching onto Jonny's wrist. "Arm day isn't over yet."

CHAPTER 2

A DINNER AT GADERO'S

A FEW MOMENTS LATER TRENT burst into the sauna with Jonny in tow. They tore off their clothes, chucking them outside the door before closing it.

Reaching for the controls, Trent set the unit and as he did, the softness of Jonny's palms started to rub against the bulk of his upper arm.

"You like that?" Trent asked him.

"Yes," Jonny said tamely, and Trent lifted his arm.

"Flex Friday," Trent said. His bicep curled into a baseball sized mound that stretched the skin seductively. Intricate veins ran across the whole thing like the back of a leaf and Jonny continued to use both sets of hands to feel each one.

As steam started to fill the room, causing them to sweat more, Jonny's dreamlike state returned. He moved his head closer to Trent's chest, burying his nose in the crease between his upper chest and neck. It smelled amazing there. Lowering a hand, he grabbed hold of Trent's erection and began to play with it, all while moving his face into Trent's armpit, then along the underside of his arm. Jonny's tongue had wormed its way out, following a deep line that separated Trent's arm muscles.

"Mmm," Trent moaned, the steam bringing his veins even further out from the surface. They were now crossing his chest, back, and legs.

Using his unattended arm, Trent rubbed the side of Jonny's torso before moving down toward his ass, kneading it with his thick fingers. He pulled away from Jonny then kneeled in front of him, licking his dick playfully before spinning the young man around. Sweat was rolling down his back, pooling in a small divot that sat at the rim of his ass. Trent rubbed his beard there, then moved downward, the prickling hairs teasing and tormenting as they went.

Now it was Jonny's turn to moan and gasp, both of which he did loudly. Trent's tongue joined the fray for a few pleasing moments before yielding to one of his fingers. It continued tantalizing him, sinking inside the hot hole until a shudder indicated that it'd found Jonny's prostrate. Once that happed, it was like the starting pistol at a race, the sole finger joined by another, then a third, and a fourth, until all were writhing with him.

Rivers of precum flowed onto the floor once Trent's thumb had entered, and a lightheadedness overcame Jonny as he felt them all moving back and forth together. Jonny dared not look back to see how much of Trent's arm was in him, but he knew that a manly fist was both abusing and rewarding that flowering hole, with an assault on his senses unlike anything he'd felt before.

"I…"

"Don't hold back, Jonny-boy."

"Ugh… I…"

Trent felt Jonny clamp down on him and he stopped moving, watching through the mist as the clear river became solid white, long strands of cum spilling out of Jonny as his cries of blissful pain filled the room.

"And with that," Trent said, slowly pulling himself out of Jonny's trembling body, "brings an end to arm day.

"WHY ARE YOU WALKING LIKE that?" Jared asked, the guest pager beeping right afterward, its red light flashing rapidly. "Oh, thank God. If your impatient pacing wasn't bad enough, J, doing it with your best duck impression was…"

Jared paused, searching for the right word but Jonny had already stopped moving, folding his arms over his luminous green *Legend of Zelda* shirt. It was one size too big, but too cool to pass up when he saw it on sale.

"I'm not walking any differently than I have for the last twenty-one years," Jonny snipped.

"Oh, so you were walking right out of the womb then?" Jared replied, giving Trent a side glance knowing that he had something to do with it.

The two gym rats stood up from the bench they'd been resting on while the restaurant prepared their seats. Jared, in his well-fitting jeans and extra-large shirt that still seemed too small, made way for the door while Trent held back, stretching in his indecently low cut black V-neck.

They'd all decided on a popular Italian place named Gadero's for their last night out. Nothing sounded better to any of them than carb-laden heaven. It was a family restaurant, lively and classy, yet informal with a whole-hearted atmosphere. They had been doing well over the years, and even with a reservation the wait had been a good thirty minutes.

"You know what I mean," Jonny said, following Jared inside.

"You *are* walking funny," Trent observed, bringing up the rear. His voice was a low whisper, but loud enough that Jared still heard.

"And it would be your fault!" Jonny hissed, trying his best to walk normally; he failed. There was a lady seated at a passing table who gave him an 'oh that poor boy, crippled at such a young age' look and Jonny waved politely at back her, then plunged his hand in a pocket, grumbling the entire time.

After being seated, the trio set about looking over the menu and ordering drinks. In addition to the waters they ordered cocktails. Jonny got himself a Long Island while Jared ordered an Negroni and Trent a whiskey neat. The drinks came and Jonny was the first to pick up his glass; he held it out in front.

"To… us," he said, and he was smiling.

Trent raised his stout glass while Jared picked his up by the narrow stem.

"To us," they said.

Their glasses touched and they drank.

As they settled back into their seats, Trent grabbed a hot roll out of the decorative basket, ripping it down the middle. Steam puffed out from it like a present and a wonderful smell filled his nostrils.

"Hey Jonny," he said coyly, holding the edges apart. "Wanna play?"

Jonny picked up another roll and threw it at Trent. He caught it mid-flight and took a massive bite out of it.

"Double fisting it I see," Jared cut in. "Just how you like it."

The three rolled with laughs when their waiter returned.

"Do you gentlemen need any extra time to look over the menu?" handsome Mediterranean man. His name was Marco (emphasis on the rolling r) and he was wearing the staff uniform: a crisp white shirt with a maroon scarf and colored accents over black trousers. "Or, perhaps you have questions for me?"

"I sure do," Trent said, "You want my number?"

Jared rubbed his eyebrow with a hooked finger, nervously waiting for Marco's response. Jonny lifted his glass and took a big swig, bulging eyes unblinking as he too waited.

Marco's look of befuddlement quickly shifted into one of amusement, then flattery. He brandished a gleaming smile that put all of theirs to shame and swiped a dark hand though his jet-black locks.

"How about I give you mine," he replied in that sexy accent and Trent couldn't manage anything more than a satisfied chuckle.

"Hell yeah, *Marrrrrco*," Trent said, pushing a messy accent. Taking the hand-written digits that were scrolled across a napkin, he pushed it into his pocket, then pointed to the menu. "We'll definitely be in touch later. Now, I *did* have another question, this time about an amazing-looking salad. Now, can this be made without the kale in it?"

"I'm sorry sir." Marco grimaced. "It's a warm kale salad so it's mixed in early in the prep process."

"Ah, then it's amazing in appearance only, just like a lot of tricks." Trent's mouth swished from side to side as he pondered other menu items. "Here's a tip from a professional bodybuilder and nutritionist, by the way: adding just a smidgen of coconut oil to that kale while it warms will help you scoop that shit right out of the pan and into the trash."

"So, the salad is a definite no?" Marco said, stifling a laugh.

"Righty, my friend," Trent said, tapping the menu. "Hmmm, I'll go ahead and take the house specialty then."

"Classic lasagna it is."

Trent nodded, taking a sip of water.

"You gents know what you want to eat?" he asked, looking at Jared and Jonny's bemused faces.

They each ordered and then had great conversations about the week leading right up to them entering the restaurant.

"I *knew* Trent was the reason you were walking funny," Jared said. He nudged Jonny on the elbow. "At least I can manage that without my fist…"

Trent's dirty look dissolved once their meals arrived, the hot plates and massive servings making him drool.

The discussions resumed and continued, between savoring the incredibly tasty food, well after the main courses were gone and dessert ordered. While waiting on the tiramisu to arrive, Jonny looked across the table from Jared to Trent and back again. A moment of silence that defied description fell over the three of them, and then Jonny realized what he was feeling. He was more at home here than at his actual home back in

Marshall. Perhaps it was just the restaurant's orange lights, continuing to serve their hearty helpings of sentiment, that made him feel that way, but he suspected – in his heart – that there was more to it than that. He felt *right,* and suspected the others felt the same way.

A screeching noise suddenly cut through the bliss.

"Hurry up and decide what you want!" a voice shrieked.

It was a middle-aged woman one table over, though for as loud as she was hissing, she might as well have been screaming in everyone's ears. She was directing her anger at a portly man in a dark suit that was struggling to contain his bulk. Seams swelled and buttons looked ready to spring off at any moment. His white shirt brought out a pallid shade of mauve along his neckline. Doing his best to ignore her, he was probably her husband, though he looked more like a prisoner. *For better or worse*, as the vows go, right?

"I've already ordered mine!" she barked, her hard features indicating that she didn't take too kindly to a cold shoulder thrust her way.

"Well, well, well," Trent said smugly, willing to help a lady in distress. He leaned over in his chair as if to get a better look, gawking at her top designer dress. He brought his second glass of whisky up to his lips, his chest bulging from the top of that insanely deep V-neck, and polished it off. "Congratulations!"

The woman glanced at him harshly, unimpressed by his physique and even less with his attire.

"And you are?" she crooned down the length of her beak-like nose.

"A man that is quite astonished. You, my dearest shrew, have managed to prove an internet meme *wrong!* Apparently, the Garden of Eden *was not* the only place a bitch knew exactly what she wanted to eat."

"Well! I never!" the woman bellowed. If she had pearls, she'd likely have clutched them.

"Never for you is probably for the best," Trent added, ending his statement with a wink. He turned his attention back to his friends, leaning against the back of his chair grinning.

"You're on rare form tonight!" Jared said, wiping away tears from the corner of his eyes. He could hear the woman blathering something indecipherable at her husband. He still hadn't ordered.

"He's been like this all week," Jonny said, also laughing.

"Not sure if I should be happy or sad that I missed it," Jared said, shaking his head.

The tiramisu arrived a short time later and Trent gave the huffing woman a gaze as he bit into the soft dessert.

"So, what are your plans for the coming weeks guys?" Trent asked, telling them that he had some clients from Hell coming in from out of country. They were apparently Russian fitness models and Trent wasn't sure he'd be able to handle them, their attitudes borderline the same as his.

"I'm sure you'll be just fine," Jonny said. "They probably need your expert help prepping for a photo shoot for some romance book covers."

"Here in little Logan?" Jared said.

"Yeah, it is picturesque," Jonny replied. He voice was laden with sadness. "I wish I could stay longer."

Jared's hand wrapped around Jonny's, giving him a light rub with his thumb.

"I know…"

"You like reading that sort of thing, Jonny-boy?" Trent asked.

"Reading what?"

"Those sex books…" he answered, a single brow cocked sexily. "I'd rather be living all that stuff, myself."

"Well, we don't all have as exciting lives as Casanova Cassidy," Jonny replied.

Jared was giggling.

"Jonny, your spring break was certainly a week worthy of a story."

"You think so?" Jonny asked, mildly surprised. But on second thought, it wasn't that surprising and Jared could be right. He returned his attention to Trent. "But to answer your question, yes, I read those kinds of books. All kinds really. I'll pretty much read any genre except historical."

"I wish I had fun reading time or training sessions with fitness models on the docket," Jared said, his face flatter than a pancake, "but I get the pleasure of finals. With midterms out of the way, they'll be here before I know it, so I'll be knee-deep in studying and coursework. Loads of fun."

"Same with me actually," Jonny said, "though my teachers this semester don't seem to be as stringent as those at LU."

"Lucky you," Jared said. "It only gets worse the further I get."

Marco reappeared like a sexy genie from a bottle, dropping off the check in its sleek black presenter.

"Take your time gents, I don't mind the fabulous eye candy …" He rolled his eyes in the direction of the still-huffing woman. "Considering *that*."

"You got it," Trent said, picking up the bill and immediately handing it over to Jared. "We'll stay for a little bit longer."

"Why do *I* get the bill?" Jared asked, seizing it.

"Because I don't pay for dinner until *after* you blow me," he answered, "and from what I recall that has yet to happen since forming this little triangle of ours."

"So, all those times we did things before…"

"All wiped clean like footprints off a beach."

"Bastard," Jared mumbled. He set the folder down, griping the entire time he was trying to fish his wallet out of his tight jeans pocket.

"You really should lay off those squats, J-rod," Trent said.

"You never complained before," Jared retorted.

During their exchange, Jonny snatched the bill off the table.

"I got this you guys," he said and before either of the others could protest, Jonny had called Marco over.

CHAPTER 3

CHILL

J ARED AND JONNY WERE RELAXING in each other's arms on the soft couch. It was just past nine o'clock, and the two were getting quite sleepy, their bellies stuffed with good food while their brains were filled with memories of great times.

Jared slid an arm across Jonny's upper back and shoulders.

"Want to watch a movie?" he asked, using his free hand to fish the remote out of the crevice at the base of the closest armrest. He turned on the television.

"Sounds good to me, though I'm not sure I'll be able to stay awake through the whole thing."

"Me either to be honest." Jared yawned. "But if I fall asleep with you here, I'm not going to complain. Oh, by the way is your alarm set?"

"For five," Jonny confirmed. "That should be okay, right?"

"Yeah. Your bus departs the station at six o'clock, so if we leave by five-forty you're good."

"Perfect," Jonny said, not wanting to dwell on the fact he was leaving in less than nine hours.

He teased the remote away from Jared, and before browsing the selections, he let his fingers rest momentarily on top of Jared's hand.

There were movies and television shows of all kinds, but a dark box near the bottom of the screen with three white Xs over it drew his attention. Jonny pressed the down arrow on the remote and navigated his way to it. These were the adult selections – basically, low budget porn. Not wanting to *watch* anything (since they were pay per view and dreadful) he *was* curious to see what was being offered. Clicking the 'OK' button, a list of sleazy tales popped up and he immediately felt dirty. That was before reading any of the captions that accompanied each listing or watching any of the sure-to-be-Oscar-worthy previews.

"What the actual fuck is up with these incestuous descriptions?" Jared asked. "'The son of a billionaire fucks his sister in the ass with her pussy?' How is that even possible?"

Jonny laughed, reading the next three and finding them equally as bad.

"Whoever is creating these captions must be from Knuckletown," Jared added.

"Haha, that must be close to Marshall," Jonny said, setting the remote on Jared's thigh. "As exciting as watching any of these would be, you know what sounds good to me?"

"What's that, babe?"

"Putting on an action-adventure with the volume low," Jonny said, moving the back of his hand across Jared's broad chest.

"Then I get to fuck you really slow…" Jared followed.

"Look at who's an amateur poet now." Jonny smiled and Jared regarded him, scratching his ever-present scruff.

"*Amateur*?" Jared said in a raspy voice. "Well, maybe as a poet but as for other things: I think not."

"Professional or not," Jonny answered, "I'm always *up* for doing some exploring with you."

With that said and before the opening credits to *Indiana Jones* were over, Jared had already taken off his shirt and jeans. His skin was illuminated in pale desert hues as Jonny's lips pecked gently on his furry chest. 'Dirty Double,' as his eight by eight cock had been so lovingly dubbed, was growing hard with excitement.

Jared returned Jonny's thoughtfulness by working a hand, then his whole arm, beneath Jonny's shirt. He lifted it and without stopping pulled until it'd been stripped all the way off. Setting the nerdy shirt over the back of the couch, Jared's fingers then teased Jonny's untidy hair before dancing across his naked skin. Starting at the neck, he traced lines downward along his taut core toward the top of Jonny's jeans.

Hooking a finger in one of the loops, Jared tugged at it twice, and Jonny unbuttoned then unzipped the denim prison.

Standing so Jared could take them off, Jonny watched as he repositioned himself, grabbing hold of each side with those muscular arms. Then, with a forceful yank the pants were down at his knees, friction burns reddening Jonny's outer thighs.

"Oh God, did that hurt?" Jared asked swiftly. He was alarmed, often forgetting his own strength.

"Not as much as my ass will be…" Jonny replied, sliding the jeans off the rest of the way. Kicking them to the side, he lifted a leg and placed a hand on Jared's shoulders for stability as he mounted him. "I l-love y-you J…" His voice stuttered and body shivered as Jared breached him.

"I love you, too," Jared whispered sweetly. They resumed kissing as he slowly pushed himself deeper inside Jonny.

Unbeknownst to them, Trent was walking into the kitchen and from the end of the master bedroom hall, through the archway into the living room, had an unobstructed view of what they were doing. Their snaking bodies were silhouettes, edged in the backlight of the eighty-inch screen. Suddenly Trent forgot that he had come to the kitchen for some water. He just stood there, watching and waiting intently.

The two were so romantic. It was something about the way they were kissing, how they were touching each other, and the way their bodies moved. They didn't look like two people fucking, but a single, amorous being. Still a foreign concept to him, Trent was learning about these new facets ever since Jonny came into the picture a week ago. He began to see there was more to life than just getting off and then moving on to the next bit of business. That was the easy part, *this* shit right here – with all the feelings and weight they carried – was the hard part. He wanted Jonny to stay and show him more.

Unaware that Trent was there and like an answer to his unspoken prayer, Jared and Jonny did just that.

The cocky motherfucker ran his fingers down his torso as he spied on them, each ab etched in flesh colored stone. Trent's hand eventually disappeared beneath the elastic of his sleep pants. Grabbing hold of his shaft, he beat it off like an alpha taking charge, studying the way Jared caressed and embraced, and the way Jonny writhed in response. The act of them exploring each other's bodies was so intimate that just witnessing it caused shiny globs that had grown fat at the end of Trent's cock to drip like a leaking faucet to the tile floor.

Suddenly, Jared grabbed hold of Jonny's hair, jerking his head backward with a gasp.

Trent stifled a moan, but a bit escaped. He picked up his pace, the slapping sound made by his balls getting louder.

Jared regarded Jonny's exposed neck, tantalizing in the faded light, and buried his face in it. Licking it along both sides, he deliberately brushed his stubble against it, causing Jonny's skin to jitter and pebble.

Trent was breathing erratically, a second hand joining his long strokes.

Jonny now ran his fingers through Jared's hair, messing it up before curling his fingers into fists that grabbed hold like the reins of a bucking bronco.

Trent was raw, his dick swollen and ready to burst. Every stroke building more pressure atop the last. He crunched forward and pointed his dick up, one last whack sending jets of cum shooting into his own mouth. The overflow spilled out in polished streaks that flowed down the length of his body, catching the light from the living room. Drenched, Trent looked over one last time, then returned to the privacy of his bedroom a moment later.

When the distant *thud* of Trent's bedroom door rose above the movie's dialogue, Jonny kissed Jared again, whispering, "He's gone. Do you think he liked it?"

"I bet he did," Jared muttered as his cock bottomed out, balls pressed between his thighs and Jonny's ass. He continued grinding. "L-looks like he… m-made a mess… and b-baby, I'm close myself…"

"Me too," Jonny said. He could feel himself building with the heat of an onrushing orgasm. It was close. "Y-you ready?"

Jared was already groaning, teeth bared as the throes of a balls-deep climax overwhelmed him. Jonny erupted with gratification a second later, panting as his cum rolled down Jared's body, collecting in wet tufts of fur along the way.

CHAPTER 4

DEPARTURE TRAIN

T HE DREADED DAY HAD FINALLY arrived. Jonny was going home.

Anxious and depressed, he woke up an hour before his alarm was due to go off, having tossed and turned uncomfortably the last fifteen minutes solid. There was a sinking feeling in his gut and he hadn't really slept much, rarely managing to do so before trips of any kind. But this time, it was the surreal reality he'd experienced all week that kept him awake. Far too potent to simply let him manufacture *make-believe* dreams, the memories of all the *real* things he'd done, and had done to him, were superior, lingering like cologne that clings to a man's shirt long after he'd taken it off.

Jonny looked up for some comfort, staring vacantly at the ceiling of Jared's bedroom. He waited. Nothing came. The ceiling was cold, mocking, and unyielding. Jonny sighed, bending an arm behind his head in a last-ditch effort to get comfortable. After all, he still had an hour to go before he *had* to be out of bed. He tried, but his arm found the pillow damp to the touch.

Have you been crying?

Blinking several times, he could feel a faint sting clinging to the rim of his eyes.

Yes, you have. My God, the week really is over, isn't it? He glanced to his left. The sheets were ruffled on Jared's side of the bed, but the area was otherwise empty. *I wonder where he went? Probably taking an early morning piss...* His bladder panged. *I should probably do the same thing...*

Jonny shifted himself into a seated position. He tried going faster but his body was stiff. Sliding his legs off the edge of the bed, his feet landed on the soft carpet while the throbbing of his bladder (*hold it...*) urged him to stand.

Hold it... hold it... hold it...

Shuffling to the bathroom (*hold it…*) he made it just in time, grabbing his flaccid penis right as it started to spew a pungent stream of dark yellow into the bowl.

"Gah that feels good," Jonny sort of whisper-muttered, relief spreading quickly.

After a quick shake (or three) and a wash of his hands, Jonny returned to the bedroom, collecting what few clothes he hadn't already packed. Folding them neatly, he set them in his suitcase, pulling out a pair of dark jeans, red underwear, and a *Yu-Gi-Oh!* shirt to wear for the journey home. He then went back into the bathroom.

As he brushed his teeth, the overhead light flickered and the bulb fizzled out while Jonny was looking at himself in the mirror. It was splattered with flecks of dried toothpaste, fresh minty foam pooling in the corners of his mouth. He spat, then rinsed out his mouth with tap water, finishing the monotonous routine by flossing his teeth as the sink sent water dribbling down the drain. Leaning over to splash warm water on his face, he added a dime-size dab of face wash to an electronic brush his mother had purchased in advance of his birthday next week. As the bristles whirred, they reminded him of Jared and Trent as he pressed them against his skin. It might have been a desperate thought, but it was a welcomed one against the dullness of real life that was starting to take over.

I wonder where Jared is? he thought, putting his toiletries in the suitcase. *Probably making coffee.*

But there was no scent of brewing coffee in the air as Jonny pulled on his underwear. He plopped down on the edge of the bed, bouncing a couple of times. His ass felt numb, conceivably a reflection of the way his soul felt while zipping up his luggage. Once the zipper stopped, it was like the week was finally over.

"I better get downstairs then," Jonny said dejectedly, planning to snag something quick to eat out of the fridge, pop the television on, and wait for either Trent or Jared to take him to the bus station.

Little did he know as he made his way downstairs – the jeans and shirt slung under one arm, the handle of the suitcase grasped with the other – that he wouldn't be doing any of those things, for there was one more surprise waiting for him.

Rounding the corner, Jonny stopped dead in his tracks, his clothes fell to the floor messily.

Trent and Jared were standing in the center of the kitchen. They were *exploring* one another with hands and lips and tongues. Jared was naked just as he had been last night while Trent was wearing the same underwear he had on when he'd first met Jonny.

Without so much as a sound, they both turned, still kissing but now staring with arms outstretched. Jonny didn't say anything either, approaching with a calm swiftness. As he got close, Jonny's arms dropped themselves to waist level, gently tracing both of their hard v-lines with his fingers. He followed Jared's with his right hand all the way down to his cock, thick and powerful, while resting his left hand just inside the elastic of Trent's underwear. He tugged at it playfully, watching as Trent's dick stretched out the fabric, remembering the musky scent as he buried his face there that first, life-changing night.

Jonny felt massive arms closing around him – Trent's right and Jared's left – locking him in their triangle. The men rubbed Jonny's shoulders, working from the outside in until they could grab each other's hands. They moved down together, stopping at the topmost part of Jonny's ass. Sliding his underwear down, they separated, spreading his cheeks apart. They continued massaging the muscle until they saw his dick pushing out against the front of his bright red undies.

Jared then kissed Jonny, and Trent kissed Jared, and Jonny kissed them both in a burst of frenzied hunger that was shared among the three men. They tasted each other's minty toothpaste and crisp mouthwash, smelled face wash infused with lemon and durable cologne, felt slick spit and soft beards.

It was then that the triangle split, Trent and Jared both pushing Jonny against the fridge. His face was pressed hard against the cold stainless steel and he could feel someone shifting his underwear down toward his ankles.

It was Trent, spreading Jonny's cheeks apart while rubbing his beard against his exposed hole. The hair tickled him mercilessly and Jonny writhed.

Jared had slid into the gap between Jonny and the fridge, and began giving him a blowjob. He worked the head with his tongue, periodically slapping the shaft against the side of his face before plunging it back into his mouth.

Jonny moaned, being worked from both ends by these muscular, god-like men.

"Jared," Trent muttered between Jonny's ass cheeks. "Table."

Suddenly, Jonny felt weightless, both Trent and Jared lifting him effortlessly as they walked toward the dining table. Setting Jonny back down, Trent set himself down on a spot that had been cleared, removing his underwear before spitting on his dick twice to work it up into a slippery missile.

Jared guided Jonny backward, impaling him on Trent's rigid dick. He moaned as Trent filled him, moving back and forth with deliberate speed.

Hooking his armed under Jonny's armpits, Trent drove himself deeper, but also angled himself backward until nearly horizontal on the table. His dick pulsed and tore into Jonny's hole.

"Still looks like there's some room in there," Jared said, pulling them both close to the table's edge.

"Oh… God…" Jonny said, almost pleading. "No, no, no…"

"You're telling me 'no'," Jared said as Trent slowed his thrusts, "but your ass is telling me 'oh fuck yes!'"

Jared spat on his cock and pressed his shaft against Trent's, its thickness hiding Trent's completely. Then, without warning he held Trent's legs firmly and started to push his dick inside *with* Trent's.

Jonny's vision and mind exploded with painful fireworks. He felt so incredibly full, on the brink of tearing completely apart.

Jared was the one moving now, his dick so big that it delivered pleasure to both Jonny's ass and, due to the tightness it was causing in the hole, to Trent's shaft as well.

"Fuck, bro," Trent said, voice ragged. "I'm about to pop."

"Damn, that feels so good Trent's reverted to being a bro," Jared said. "Go for it…"

Trent complied, his load surging into Jonny's ass, churned into a pasty white batter by Jared's thick rod, which had far more torment planned.

Jonny let out a whimper that was damn close to tears.

"Oh God…" he cried, cum starting to ooze out from his hard dick.

"Fuck him," Jared ordered, pulling his cock out.

Jonny felt a tremendous rush of relief, like water in a tub that had one of those old-fashioned stoppers pulled.

Jared helped Jonny down. He was wobbling and Trent flipped himself over on the table.

Spinning around, Jonny plunged his drooling dick into Trent's ass, moving back and forth slowly so he didn't get off right away. Oh, he was on the brink alright, but riding the edge *this* close felt fucking amazing.

Jonny thought he could have managed a few more minutes, but Jared had other plans. He rammed himself into Jonny's ass while he was still fucking Trent and within a few skin-splitting pumps, Jonny couldn't hold back any longer, sending his cum deep into Trent's hole. There was so much of it that it leaked out onto the tabletop and floor.

"You better keep riding this train," Jared said, slapping Jonny's ass with an open palm before latching hold of his waist.

A red handprint started to form on Jonny's milky skin and his legs were trembling. He buckled but Jared's powerful grip kept him up, right where he needed to be.

"Almost there," Jared said after a few more long pumps. Pulling out, his veined dick pulsed. Thick ropes shot across Jonny's ass, back, even his neck, splashing droplets of cum into his brown hair.

Jonny collapsed onto Trent, his body shuddering as they kissed.

Jared was still shooting, and once the last spurt oozed out from his monstrous cock, he laid it between Jonny's ass cheeks and looked proudly at his handiwork.

"Fuck that's a mess," he said, so low it was incoherent to the others. "Always looking like a damn glazed donut."

Trent and Jonny didn't care, resting in their respective positions for a few minutes. The quiet was bliss.

Trent was the first to break the silence.

"Well, you've caused me to break my rules in the house, Jonny-boy. I'm not sure I can look at myself in the mirror anymore."

"Sure, you can," Jonny said with a laugh. "You're just knocked down a peg or two."

"There's a reason I set up that rule in the first place, though," Trent said.

"Oh?"

"Yeah, because there's no cleaning lady to come and wipe up his mess," Jared answered on his behalf. "Poor Lisa. I hope you're paying her well, T-bag."

"I pay her well enough."

"In cash or dick?" Jonny joked.

Jared laughed. Trent didn't.

"Yeah, yeah, look at Mr. Jonny Smartass over here. Thinks he has the big balls now that he's had a piece." Trent raised a middle finger, waving it around so he was sure both of them could see it. "Damn you and this J-effect, man. Damn you."

All three chuckled and started to get up from the table.

"I'm so glad I found you guys," Jonny said.

"Same here," Jared said.

Trent just grunted, wiping some stray spit from his beard.

"I *really* don't want this to end guys," Jonny said, walking over to the paper towel rack. He ripped one off and dabbed it around his body.

"What am I going to do without seeing you every day?"

"Suffer," said Trent plainly.

"Be bored," said Jared at once.

"Well thanks, you two pieces of shit."

"Hey now," Trent said innocently, "such language."

A mischievous twinkle formed in his eyes.

"Oh gosh, what do you have planned, man?" Jared asked cautiously.

As always, Trent's cock seemed to grow when he had that look in his eyes. He lowered a hand, grabbing hold of the base before giving it a long, tender stroke.

"Well," he said casually, already teasing a strand of precum out of the tip, "you *do* realize that Memorial Day weekend is just a couple months away? After that, it's an eternity before your next semesters kick off…"

Jonny and Jared considered what Tent was saying, glancing at each other with hearts beating hard and fast in their chests. Huge smiles spread across their faces, gleaming brighter than the sun. Suddenly, the storm cloud that was thundering above their goodbyes disappeared, letting the three of them know that everything was going to be okay.

THE END